B
Q

# TOBIAS WOLFF

## Two Boys and a Girl

A
BLOOMSBURY
QUID

This story first appeared in *Antaeus* magazine, 1995

First published in Great Britain 1996

Copyright © 1995, 1996 by Tobias Wolff

The moral right of the author has been asserted

Bloomsbury Publishing Plc,
2 Soho Square, London W1V 6HB

A CIP catalogue record for this book
is available from the British Library

ISBN 0 7475 2892 6

Typeset by Hewer Text Composition Services, Edinburgh
Printed by St Edmundsbury Press, Suffolk
Jacket design by Jeff Fisher

Gilbert saw her first. This was in late
June, at a party. She was sitting alone
in the back yard, stretched out on a
lawn chair, when he went to get a
beer from the cooler. He tried to
think of something to say to her but
she seemed complete in her solitude
and he was afraid of sounding intru-
sive and obvious. Later he saw her
again, inside – a pale, dark-haired girl
with dark eyes and lipstick smears on
her teeth. She was dancing with
Gilbert's best friend, Rafe. The night
after that she was with Rafe when he

picked Gilbert up to go to another party, and again the night after that. Her name was Mary Ann.

Mary Ann, Rafe, and Gilbert. They went everywhere together that summer, to parties and movies and the lake, to the pools of friends, and on long aimless drives after Gilbert got off work at his father's bookstore. Gilbert didn't have a car, so Rafe did the driving; his grandfather had given him his immaculate old Buick convertible as a reward for getting into Yale. Mary Ann leaned against him with her bare white feet up on the dash while Gilbert sprawled like a pasha in the back and handed out the beers and made ironic comment on whatever attracted his notice.

Gilbert was very ironic. At the high

school where he and Rafe had been
classmates, the yearbook editors voted
him 'most cynical'. That pleased him.
Gilbert believed disillusionment to be
the natural consequence, even the
duty, of a mind that could cut through
the authorised version to the true
nature of things. He made it his business to take nothing on trust, to respect
no authority but that of his own
judgment, and to be elegantly un-
surprised at the grossest crimes and
follies, especially those of the world's
anointed.

Mary Ann listened to what he said,
even when she seemed to be occupied
with Rafe. Gilbert knew this, and he
knew when he'd managed to shock
her. She clenched her hands, blinked
rapidly, and a red splotch, vivid as a

birthmark, appeared on the milky skin of her neck. It wasn't hard to shock Mary Ann. Her father, a captain in the Coast Guard, was the squarest human being Gilbert had ever met. One night when he and Rafe were waiting for Mary Ann, Captain McCoy stared at Gilbert's sandals and asked what he thought about the beatniks. Mrs McCoy had doilies all over the house, and pictures of kittens and the Holy Land and dogs playing poker, and in the toilets these chemical gizmos that turned the water blue. Whenever Gilbert took a leak at Mary Ann's house he felt sorry for her.

In August Rafe went fishing in Canada with his father. He left Gilbert the keys to the Buick and told him to take care of Mary Ann. Gilbert recognised this as what the hero of a war movie says to his drab sidekick before leaving on the big mission.

Rafe delivered his instructions while he was in his room packing for the trip. Gilbert lounged on the bed watching him. He wanted to talk but Rafe was playing his six-record set of *I Pagliacci*, which Gilbert didn't believe he really liked, though Rafe made occasional humming noises as if he knew the whole score by heart. Gilbert thought he was taking up opera the same way he'd taken up squash that winter, as an accessory. He lay back and was silent. Rafe went about his business: he was graceful and precise, and he assembled his gear without waste of motion or any hesitation as to where things were. At one point he walked over to the

mirror and studied himself as if he were
alone, and Gilbert was surprised by the
anger he felt. Then Rafe turned to him
and tossed the keys on the bed and
spoke his line about taking care of
Mary Ann.

The next day Gilbert drove the
Buick around town all by himself. He
double-parked in front of Nordstrom's
with the top down and smoked cigarettes and watched the women come
out as if he were waiting for one of
them. Now and then he examined his
watch and frowned. He drove on to a
pier at the wharf and waved at one of
the passengers on the boat to Victoria.
She was looking down at the water and
didn't see him until she raised her eyes as
the boat was backing out of the slip and
caught him blowing a kiss at her. She

stepped away from the rail and vanished from sight. Later he went to La Luna, a bar near the university where he knew he wouldn't get carded, and took a seat from which he could see the Buick. When the bar filled up he walked outside and raised the hood and checked the oil, right in front of La Luna's big picture window. To a couple walking past he said, 'This damn thing drinks oil like it's going out of style.' Then he drove off with the expression of a man with important and not entirely pleasant business to perform. He stopped and bought cigarettes in two different drugstores. He called home from the second drugstore and told his mother he wouldn't be in for dinner and asked if he'd gotten any mail. No, his mother said, nothing. Gilbert ate at a

drive-in and cruised for a while and
then went up to the lookout above
Alki Point and sat on the hood of the
Buick and smoked in a moody, philo-
sophical way, deliberately ignoring the
girls with their dates in the cars around
him. A heavy mist stole in from the
sound. Across the water the lights of the
city blurred, and a foghorn began to call.
Gilbert flipped his cigarette into the
shadows and rubbed his bare arms.
When he got home he called Mary
Ann, and it was agreed that they would
go to a movie the following night.

After the movie Gilbert drove Mary
Ann back to her house, but instead of
getting out of the car she sat where she
was and they went on talking. It was
easy, easier than he had imagined.

When Rafe was with them Gilbert could speak through him to Mary Ann and be witty or deep or out-rageous. But in the moments they'd been alone, waiting for Rafe to rejoin them, he had always found himself tongue-tied, in a kind of panic. He'd cudgel his brains for something to say, and whatever he did come up with sounded tense and sharp. But that didn't happen, not that night.

It was raining hard. When Gilbert saw that Mary Ann wasn't in any hurry to get out, he cut the engine and they sat there in the faint marine light of the radio-tuning band with liquid shadows playing over their faces from the rain streaming down the windows. The rain drummed in gusts on the canvas roof but inside it was warm and close, like a tent during a storm. Mary Ann was talking about nursing school, about her fear that she wouldn't measure up in the tough courses, especially Anatomy and Physiology. Gilbert thought she was being ritually humble and said, Oh, come on, you'll do fine.

I don't know, she said. I just don't know. And then she told him how badly she'd done in Science and Maths, and how two of her teachers had personally gone down to the nursing-school admissions office to help her get in. Gilbert saw that she really was afraid of failing, and that she had reason to be afraid. Now that she'd said so herself, it made sense to him that she struggled in school. She wasn't quick that way; wasn't clever. There was a simplicity about her.

She leaned back into the corner, watching the rain. She looked sad. Gilbert thought of touching her cheek with the back of his hand to reassure her. He waited a moment, then told her it wasn't exactly true that he was trying to make up his mind whether to go to the University of Washington or Amherst. He should have corrected that misunderstanding before. The actual truth was, he hadn't gotten into Amherst. He'd made it on to the waiting list, but with only three weeks left until school began he figured his odds were just about nil.

She turned and regarded him. He couldn't see her eyes. They were dark pools with only a glint of light at the bottom. She asked why he hadn't gotten in.

To this question Gilbert had no end of answers. He thought of new ones every day, and he was sick of them all. I stopped working, he said. I just completely slacked off.

But you should have gotten in wherever you wanted. You're smart enough.

I talk a pretty good game, I guess. He took out a cigarette and tapped the end against the steering wheel. I don't know why I smoke these damn things, he said.

You like the way they make you look. Intellectual.

I guess. He lit it.

She watched him closely as he took the first drag. Let me, she said. Just a puff.

Their fingers touched when he
handed her the cigarette.

You're going to be a great nurse, he
said.

She took a puff of the cigarette and
blew the smoke out slowly.

Neither of them spoke for a time.

I'd better go in, she said.

Gilbert watched her go up the walkway to her house. She didn't hunch
and run but moved sedately through
the lashing rain as if this were a night
like any other. He waited until he saw
her step inside, then turned the radio
back up and drove away. He kept
tasting her lipstick on the cigarette.

When he called from work the next
day her mother answered and asked
him to wait. Mary Ann was out of

breath when she came to the phone. She said she'd been outside on a ladder, helping her dad paint the house. What are you up to? she asked.

I was just wondering what you were doing, he said.

He took her to La Luna that night, and the next. Both times they got the same booth, right near the jukebox. 'Don't Think Twice, It's Alright' had just come out and Mary Ann played it again and again while they talked. On the third night some guys in baseball uniforms were sitting there when they came in. Gilbert was annoyed and saw that she was, too. They sat at the bar for a time but kept getting jostled by the drinkers behind them. They decided to go someplace else. Gilbert was paying his tab when the baseball players stood up to leave, and Mary Ann slipped into the booth just ahead of an older couple who'd been waiting nearby.

We were here first, the woman said to Mary Ann as Gilbert sat down across from her.

This is our booth, Mary Ann said, in a friendly, informative way.

How do you figure that?

Mary Ann looked at the woman as if she'd asked a truly eccentric question. Well, I don't know, she said. It just is.

Afterwards it kept coming back to Gilbert, the way Mary Ann had said 'our booth'. He collected such observations and pondered them when he was away from her: her breathlessness when she came to the phone, the habit she'd formed of taking puffs from his cigarettes and helping herself to his change to play the jukebox, the way she listened to him, with such open credulity that he found it impossible to brag or make excuses or say things merely for effect. He couldn't be facetious with Mary Ann, she always thought he meant exactly what he said, and then he had to stop and try to explain that he'd actually meant something else. His irony began to sound weak and somehow envious. It sounded thin and unmanly.

Mary Ann gave him no occasion for it. She took him seriously. She wrote down the names of the books he spoke of – *On the Road*, *The Stranger*, *The Fountainhead*, and some others that he hadn't actually read but knew about and intended to read as soon as he found the time. She listened when he explained what was wrong with Barry Goldwater and *Reader's Digest* and the television shows she liked, and agreed that he was probably right. In the solemnity of her attention he heard himself saying things he had said to no one else, confessing hopes so implausible he had barely confessed them to himself. He was often surprised by his own honesty. But he stopped short of telling Mary Ann what was most on his mind, and what he believed she already knew, because of the chance that she didn't know or wasn't ready to admit she did. Once he said it, everything would change, for all of them, and he wasn't prepared to risk this.

They went out every night but two, once when Gilbert had to work overtime and once when Captain McCoy took Mary Ann and her mother to dinner. They saw a couple more movies and went to a party and to La Luna and drove around the city. The nights were warm and clear and Gilbert put the top down and poked along in the right lane. He used to wonder, with some impatience, why Rafe drove so slowly. Now he knew. To command the wheel of an open car with a girl on the seat beside you was to be established in a condition that only a fool would hasten to end. He drove slowly around the lake and downtown and up to the lookouts and then back to Mary Ann's house. The first few nights they sat in the car. After that, Mary Ann invited Gilbert inside.

He talked; she talked. She talked

about her little sister, Kathleen, who had died of cystic fibrosis two years before, and whose long hard dying had brought her family close and given her the idea of becoming a nurse. She talked about friends from school and the nuns who had taught her. She talked about her parents and grandparents and Rafe. All her talk was of her affections. Unconditional enthusiasm generally had a wearying effect on Gilbert, but not on these nights with Mary Ann. She gave praise, it seemed to him, not to shine it back on herself or to dissemble some secret bitterness but because that was her nature. That was how she was, and he liked her for it, as he liked it that she didn't question everything but trusted freely, like a child.

She had been teaching herself the
guitar and sometimes she would con-
sent to play and sing for him, old
ballads about mine disasters and nice
lads getting hanged for poaching and
noblewomen drowning their babies.
He could see how the words moved
her: so much that her voice would
give out for moments at a time, during
which she would bite her lower lip
and gaze down at the floor. She put
folk songs on the record player and
listened to them with her eyes closed.
She also liked Roy Orbison and the
Fleetwoods and Ray Charles. One
night she was bringing some fudge
from the kitchen just as 'Born to
Lose' came on. Gilbert stood and
offered his hand with a dandified
flourish that she could have laughed

off if she'd chosen to. She put the plate down and took his hand and they began to dance, stiffly at first, from a distance, then easily and close. They fitted perfectly. Perfectly. He felt the rub of her hips and thighs, the heat of her skin. Her warm hand tightened in his. He breathed in the scent of lavender water with the sunny smell of her hair and the faint salt smell of her body. He breathed it all in again and again. And then he felt himself grow hard and rise against her, so that she had to know, she just had to know, and he waited for her to move away. But she did not move away. She pressed close to him until the song ended, and for a moment or two after. Then she stepped back and let go of Gilbert's hand and in a hoarse voice asked him if he wanted some fudge. She was facing him but managing not to look at him.

Maybe later, he said, and held out his hand again. May I have the honour?

She walked over to the couch and sat down. I'm so clumsy.

No you're not. You're a great dancer.

She shook her head.

He sat down in the chair across from her. She still wouldn't look at him. She put her hands together and stared at them.

Then she said, How come Rafe's dad picks on him all the time?

I don't know. There isn't any particular reason. Bad chemistry, I guess.

It's like he can't do anything right. His dad won't let him alone, even when I'm there. I bet he's having a miserable time.

It was true that neither Rafe's father nor his mother could take any pleasure in their son. Gilbert had no idea why this should be so. But it was a strange subject to have boiled up out of nowhere like this, and for her to be suddenly close to tears about. Don't worry about Rafe, he said. Rafe can take care of himself.

The grandfather clock chimed the Westminster Bells, then struck twelve times. The clock had been made to go with the living-room ensemble and its tone, tinny and untrue, set Gilbert on edge. The whole house set him on edge: the pictures, the matching Colonial furniture, the single bookshelf full of condensed books. It was like a house

Russian spies would practise being Americans in.

It's just so unfair, Mary Ann said. Rafe is so sweet.

He's a good egg, Rafe, Gilbert said. Most assuredly. One of the best.

He is the best.

Gilbert got up to leave and Mary Ann did look at him then, with something like alarm. She stood and followed him outside, on to the porch. When he looked back from the end of the walkway she was watching him with her arms crossed over her chest. Call me tomorrow, she said. OK?

I was thinking of doing some reading, he said. Then he said, I'll see. I'll see how things go.

\*     \*     \*

The next night they went bowling.
This was Mary Ann's idea. She was a
good bowler and frankly out to win.
Whenever she got a strike she threw
her head back and gave a great bark
of triumph. She questioned Gilbert's
score-keeping until he got rattled and
told her to take over, which she did
without even a show of protest. When
she guttered her ball she claimed she'd
slipped on a wet spot and insisted on
bowling that frame again. He didn't let
her, he understood that she would
despise him if he did, but her shame-
lessness somehow made him happier
than he'd been all day.

As he pulled up to her house Mary
Ann said, Next time I'll give you some
pointers. You could be half decent if
you knew what you were doing.

He heard that 'next time'. He killed the engine and turned and looked at her. Mary Ann, he said.

He had never said so much before.

She looked straight ahead and didn't answer. Then she said, I'm thirsty. You want a glass of juice or something? Before Gilbert could say anything, she added, We'll have to sit outside, OK? I think we woke up my dad last night.

Gilbert waited on the steps while Mary Ann went into the house. Paint cans and brushes were arranged on top of the porch railing. Captain McCoy scraped and painted one side of the house every year. This year he was doing the front. That was just like him, to eke it out one side at a time. Gilbert had once helped the Captain make crushed ice for drinks. The way

the Captain did it, he held a single cube
in his hand and clobbered it with a
hammer until it was pulverised. Then
another cube. Then another. Etcetera.
When Gilbert wrapped a whole tray's
worth in a hand towel and started to
bang it on the counter the Captain
grabbed the towel away from him.
That's not how you do it! he said. He
found Gilbert another hammer and the
two of them stood there hitting cube
after cube.

Mary Ann came out with two glasses
of orange juice. She sat beside Gilbert
and they drank and looked out at the
Buick gleaming under the streetlight.

I'm off tomorrow, Gilbert said. You
want to go for a drive?

Gee, I wish I could. I promised my
dad I'd paint the fence.

We'll paint, then.

That's all right. It's your day off. You should do something.

Painting's something.

Something you like, dummy.

I like to paint. In fact I love to paint. Gilbert.

No kidding, I love to paint. Ask my folks. Every free minute, I'm out there with a brush.

Like fun.

So what time do we start? Look, it's only been three hours since I did my last fence and already my hand's starting to shake.

Stop it! I don't know. Whenever. After breakfast.

He finished his juice and rolled the glass between his hands. Mary Ann.

He felt her hesitate. Yes?

He kept rolling the glass. What do your folks think about us going out so much?

They don't mind. I think they're glad, actually.

I'm not exactly their type.

*Hah.* You can say that again.

What're they so glad about, then?

You're not Rafe.

What, they don't like Rafe?

Oh, they like him, a lot. A whole lot. They're always saying how if they had a son, and so on. But my dad thinks we're getting too serious.

Ah. Too serious. So I'm comic relief.

Don't say that.

I'm not comic relief?

No.

Gilbert put his elbows on the step

behind him. He looked up at the sky and said, carefully, He'll be back in a couple of days.

I know.

Then what?

She leaned forward and stared into the yard as if she'd heard a sound.

He waited for a time, aware of every breath he took. Then what? he said again.

I don't know. Maybe . . . I don't know. I'm really kind of tired. You're coming tomorrow, right?

If that's what you want.

You said you were coming tomorrow.

Only if you want me to.

I want you to.

OK. Sure. Tomorrow, then.

\*     \*     \*

Gilbert stopped at a diner on the way home. He ate a piece of apple pie, then drank coffee and watched the cars go past. To an ordinary person driving by he supposed he must look pretty tragic, sitting here alone over a coffee cup, cigarette smoke curling past his face. And the strange thing was, that person would be right. He was about to betray his best friend. He was about to cut Rafe off from the two people he trusted most, possibly, he understood, from trust itself. Himself, too, he would betray – his belief, held deep under the stream of his flippancy, that he was steadfast and loyal. And he knew what he was doing. That was why this whole thing was tragic, because he knew what he was doing and could not do otherwise.

He had thought it all out. He could give himself reasons. Rafe and Mary Ann would have broken up anyway, sooner or later. Rafe was moving on. He didn't know it, but he was leaving them behind. He'd have roommates, guys from rich families who'd invite him home for vacation, take him skiing, sailing. He'd wear a tuxedo to debutante parties where he'd meet girls from Smith and Mt. Holyoke, philosophy majors, English majors, girls with ideas who were reading the same books he was reading and other books, too, who could say things he wouldn't have expected them to say. He'd get interested in one of these girls and go on road trips with his friends to her college. She'd come to New Haven. They'd rendezvous in Boston, New

York. He'd meet her parents. And on
the first day of his next trip home,
honourable Rafe would enter Mary
Ann's house and leave half an hour
later with a sorrowful face and a heart
leaping with joy. There wouldn't be
many more trips home, not after that.
What was here to bring him all that
way? Not his parents, those crocodiles.
Not Mary Ann. Himself? Good old
Gilbert? Please.

And Mary Ann, what about Mary
Ann? When Rafe double-timed her
and then dropped her cold, what
would happen to that simple good-
heartedness of hers? Would she begin
to suspect it, stand guard over it? He
was right to do anything to keep that
from happening.

These were the reasons, and they

were good reasons, but Gilbert could
not make use of them. He knew that he
would do what he was going to do
even if Rafe stayed at home and went
to college with him, or if Mary Ann
was somewhat more calculating. Reasons always came with a purpose, to
give the appearance of struggle between principle and desire. But
there'd been no struggle. Principle
had power only until you found what
you had to have.

Captain McCoy was helping Mrs
McCoy into the car when Gilbert
pulled up behind him. The Captain
waited as his wife gathered her dress
inside, then closed the door and walked
back toward the Buick. Gilbert came
around to meet him.

TOBIAS WOLFF

Mary Ann tells me you're going to help with the fence.

Yes, sir.

There's not that much of it — shouldn't take too long.

They both looked at the fence, about sixty feet of white pickets that ran along the sidewalk. Mary Ann came out on the porch and mimed the word Hi.

Captain McCoy said, Would you mind picking up the paint? It's that Glidden store down on California. Just give 'em my name. He opened his car door, then looked at the fence again. Scrape her good. That's the secret. Give her a good scraping and the rest'll go easy. And try not to get any paint on the grass.

Mary Ann came through the gate

37

and waved as her parents drove off. She said that they were going over to Bremerton to see her grandmother. Well, she said. You want some coffee or something?

I'm fine.

He followed her up the walk. She had on cut-offs. Her legs were very white and they flexed in a certain way as she climbed the porch steps. Captain McCoy had set out two scrapers and two brushes on the railing, all four of them exactly parallel. Mary Ann handed Gilbert a scraper and they went back to the fence. What a day! she said. Isn't it the most beautiful day? She knelt to the right of the gate and began to scrape. Then she looked back at Gilbert watching her and said, Why don't you do that side

38

over there? We'll see who gets done first.

There wasn't much to scrape, some blisters, a few peeling patches here and there. This fence is in good shape, Gilbert said. How come you're painting it?

It goes with the front. When we paint the front, we always paint the fence.

It doesn't need it. All it needs is some retouching.

I guess. Dad wanted us to paint it, though. He always paints it when he paints the front.

Gilbert stopped, looked behind him at the gleaming white house, the bright weedless lawn trimmed to the nap of a crewcut.

Guess who called this morning, Mary Ann said.

Who?

Rafe! There was a big storm coming in so they left early. He'll be back tonight. He sounded really great. He said to say hi.

Gilbert ran the scraper up and down a picket.

It was so good to hear his voice, Mary Ann said. I wish you'd been here to talk to him.

A kid went by on a bicycle, cards snapping against the spokes.

We should do something, Mary Ann said. Surprise him. Maybe we could take the car over to the house, be waiting out front when he gets back. Wouldn't that be great?

I wouldn't have any way to get home.

Rafe can give you a ride.

Gilbert sat back and watched Mary Ann. She was halfway down her section of the fence. He waited for her to turn and face him. Instead she bent over to work at a spot near the ground. Her hair fell forward, exposing the nape of her neck. Maybe you could invite someone along, Mary Ann said.

Invite someone. What do you mean, a girl?

Sure. It would be nice if you had a girl. It would be perfect.

Gilbert threw the scraper against the fence. He saw Mary Ann freeze. It would *not* be perfect, he said. When she still didn't turn around he stood and went up the walk and through the house to the kitchen. He paced back and forth. He went to the sink, drank a glass of water, and stood with his hands on the counter. He saw what Mary Ann was thinking of, the two of them sitting in the open car, herself jumping out as Rafe pulled up, the wild embrace. Rafe unshaven, reeking of smoke and nature, a little abashed at all this emotion in front of his father but pleased, too, and amused. And all the while Gilbert looking coolly on, hands in his pockets, ready to say the sly mocking words that would tell Rafe that all was as before. That was how she saw it going. As if nothing had happened.

Mary Ann had just about finished her section when Gilbert came back outside. I'll go get the paint, he told her. I don't think there's much left to scrape on my side, but you can take a look.

She stood and tried to smile. Thank you, she said.

He saw that she had been in tears, and this did not soften him but confirmed him in his purpose.

Mary Ann had already spread out the tarp, pulling one edge under the fence so the drips wouldn't fall on the grass. When Gilbert opened the can she laughed and said, Look! They gave you the wrong colour.

No, that's exactly the right colour.

But it's *red*. We need white. Like it is now.

You don't want to use white, Mary Ann. Believe me.

She frowned.

Red is the perfect colour for this. No

offence, but white is the worst choice you could make.

But the house is white.

*Exactly*, Gilbert said. So are the houses next door. You put a white fence here, what you end up with is complete boredom. It's like being in a hospital, you know what I mean?

I don't know. I guess it is a lot of white.

What the red will do, the red will give some contrast and pick up the bricks in the walk. It's just what you want here.

Well, maybe. The thing is, I don't think I should. Not this time. Next time, maybe, if my dad wants to.

Look. Mary Ann. What your dad wants is for you to use your own head.

44

Mary Ann squinted at the fence.

He said, You have to trust me on this, OK?

She sucked in her lower lip, then nodded. OK. If you're sure.

Gilbert dipped his brush. The world's bland enough already, right? Everyone's always talking about the banality of evil – what about the evil of banality?

They painted through the morning and into the afternoon. Every now and then Mary Ann would back off a few steps and take in what they'd done. At first she kept her thoughts to herself. The more they painted, the more she had to say. Toward the end she went out into the street and stood there with her hands on her hips. It's interesting, isn't it? Really different. I see what you

mean about picking up the bricks. It's
pretty red, though.

It's perfect.

Think my dad'll like it?

Your dad? He'll be crazy about it.

Think so? Gilbert? Really?

Wait till you see his face.

# A NOTE ON THE AUTHOR

Tobias Wolff is the author of the short story collections *Hunters in the Snow* and *Back in the World*, and two memoirs, *This Boy's Life* and *In Pharaoh's Army*. His most recent collection of stories is *The Night in Question*. He lives in Syracuse.

Margaret Atwood          *The Labrador Fiasco*
T. Coraghessan Boyle     *She Wasn't Soft*
Nadine Gordimer          *Harald, Claudia, and their Son Duncan*
David Guterson           *The Drowned Son*
Jay McInerney            *The Queen and I*
Candia McWilliam         *Change of Use*
Will Self                *A Story for Europe*
Patrick Süskind          *Maître Mussard's Bequest*
Joanna Trollope          *Faith*

# AVAILABLE AS BLOOMSBURY CLASSICS

## AVAILABLE AS BLOOMSBURY POETRY CLASSICS

Selected poetry of Matthew Arnold
Selected poetry of William Blake
Selected poetry of Rupert Brooke
Selected poetry of Elizabeth Barrett Browning
Selected poetry of Robert Browning
Selected poetry of Robert Burns
Selected poetry of Lord Byron
Selected poetry of John Clare
Selected poetry of Samuel Taylor Coleridge
Selected poetry of Emily Dickinson
Selected poetry of John Donne
Selected poetry of John Dryden
Selected poetry of Thomas Hardy
Selected poetry of Robert Herrick
Selected poetry of Gerard Manley Hopkins
Selected poetry of John Keats
Selected poetry of Rudyard Kipling
Selected poetry of D. H. Lawrence
Selected poetry of Andrew Marvell
Selected poetry of John Milton
Selected poetry of Wilfred Owen
Selected poetry of Alexander Pope
Selected poetry of Christina Rossetti
Selected poetry of Walter Scott
Selected poetry of William Shakespeare
Selected poetry of P. B. Shelley
Selected poetry of Alfred Lord Tennyson
Selected poetry of Edward Thomas
Selected poetry of Walt Whitman
Selected poetry of Oscar Wilde
Selected poetry of William Wordsworth
Selected poetry of W. B. Yeats